For Desma

ALADDIN

An imprint of Simon & Schuster Children's Publishing Division
1230 Avenue of the Americas, New York, New York 10020
First Aladdin hardcover edition November 2016
Copyright © 2016 by Chad J. Thompson
All rights reserved, including the right of reproduction in whole or in part in any form.
ALADDIN is a trademark of Simon & Schuster, Inc., and related logo is a registered trademark of Simon & Schuster, Inc.
For information about special discounts for bulk purchases, please contact Simon & Schuster Special Sales at
1-866-506-1949 or business@simonandschuster.com.
The Simon & Schuster Speakers Bureau can bring authors to your live event. For more information or
to book an event contact the Simon & Schuster Speakers Bureau
at 1-866-248-3049 or visit our website at www.simonspeakers.com.
Designed by Karina Granda
The illustrations for this book were rendered digitally.
The text of this book was set in Bliss and Candy Square.
Manufactured in China 0816 SCP
2 4 6 8 10 9 7 5 3 1
Library of Congress Control Number 2015959004
ISBN 978-1-4814-7095-7 (hc)
ISBN 978-1-4814-7096-4 (eBook)

Rhymes with Doug

written and illustrated by
CHAD J. THOMPSON

ALADDIN   New York   London   Toronto   Sydney   New Delhi

See you tomorrow, Doug.

Ooh, look. You have
a package.

Otto, the Amazing Rhyming Bird.

Be careful what you say.

Very dangerous.

Well, aren't you the cutest little thing?

Hello, Otto.

My name is Doug.

You can talk!

A talking bird!

Awesome!

What else can you say?

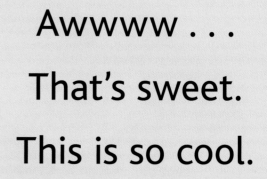

Awwww . . .
That's sweet.
This is so cool.

You're not dangerous at all, are you, Otto?

A puppy!

Thanks, Otto.

A talking bird and a new puppy.

This is the best day of my life!

Whoa, whoa, whoa!!

This is not okay.

Change me back, Otto.

Change me baaa . . .

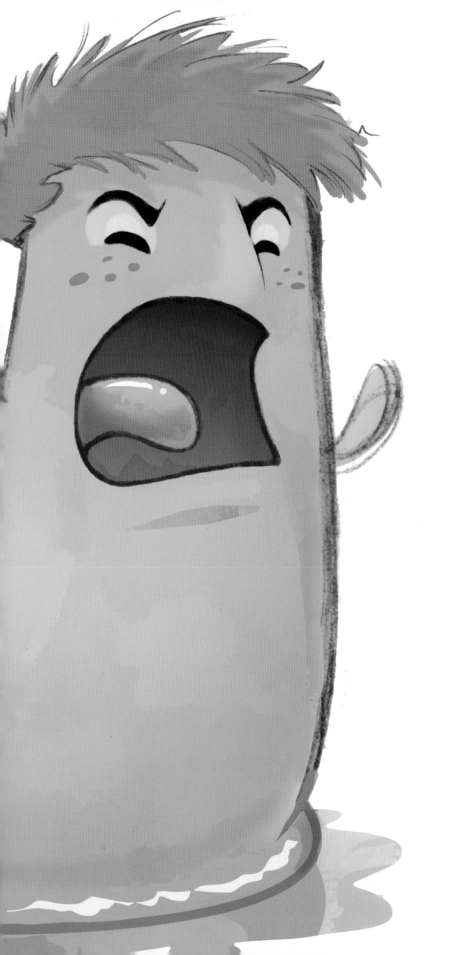

Oh, come on.

I have a test tomorrow, Otto.

I can't go to school like this.

Hurry up before my mom sees me.

This is the worst day of my life.

This isn't helping, Otto.

Oh! Now what?

Woo-hoo!

Okay, now stop.

Stop. Stop! STOP!

Otto! Quick,

say something else.

Say something else. . . .

JUG?

PLUG?

TUG?

Hurry, Otto!

Thank goodness.

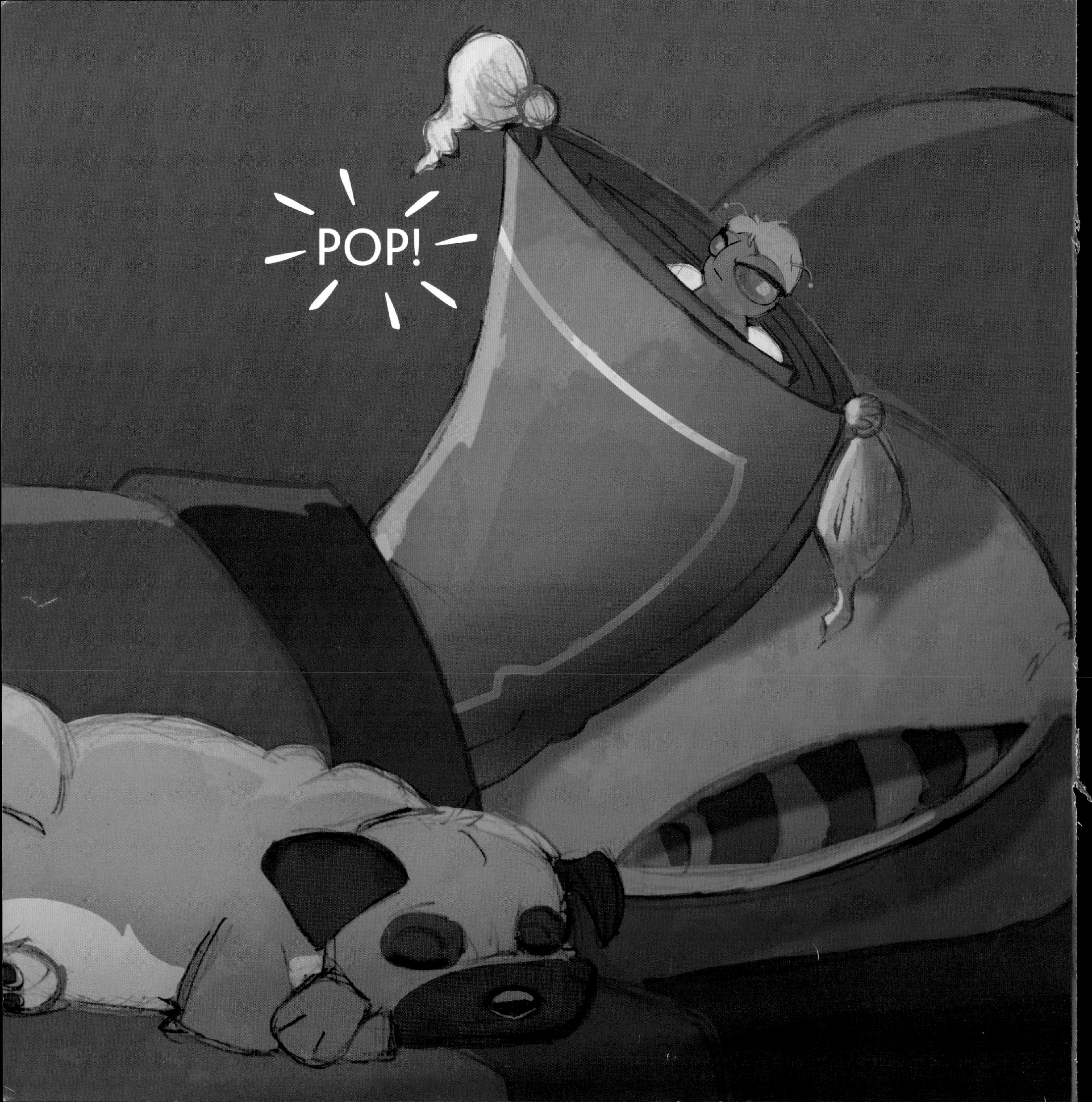
POP!